To Alexa Karrodie

[signature]

3/7/2002

MASTER MAID

A TALE OF NORWAY

RETOLD BY
AARON SHEPARD

PICTURES BY
PAULINE ELLISON

Dial Books for Young Readers
New ★ York

Published by Dial Books for Young Readers
A Division of Penguin Books USA Inc.
375 Hudson Street
New York, New York 10014
Text copyright © 1997 by Aaron Shepard
Pictures copyright © 1997 by Pauline Ellison
All rights reserved
Designed by Atha Tehon
Printed in Hong Kong on acid-free paper
First Edition
1 3 5 7 9 10 8 6 4 2

Library of Congress Cataloging in Publication Data
Shepard, Aaron.
Master Maid: a tale of Norway
retold by Aaron Shepard: pictures by Pauline Ellison.
p.   cm.
Includes bibliographical references.
Summary: A stubborn young prince goes to work for an evil troll
where he falls in love with a captive maiden.
ISBN 0-8037-1821-7 (trade).—ISBN 0-8037-1822-5 (library)
[1. Fairy tales.   2. Folklore—Norway.]   I. Ellison, Pauline, ill.   II. Title.
PZ8.S3425Mas   1997   398.2'0948102—dc20   [E]
94-37527   CIP   AC

The art for this book was prepared using watercolor paints.
It was then color-separated and reproduced in full color.

For Dawn A.S.

For Nina P.E.

About the Story

The Norwegian tale "Mastermaid" is found in the collection of the great 19th-century folklorists Peter Asbjornsen and Jorgen Moe. Classified in the Aarne-Thompson index as "The Girl as Helper in the Hero's Flight" (tale type #313), this is one of the finest versions of a tale known on every continent, and even told in ancient Greece as the myth of Jason and Medea.

The original story is much longer than this retelling and relates further adventures of Leif and Master Maid after their escape from the troll. It appears in many collections, including *Folktales of Norway*, edited by Reidar Christiansen, University of Chicago Press, 1964, and *East o' the Sun & West o' the Moon*, translated by George Webbe Dasent, Dover, New York, 1970.

Leif is pronounced "Leef." *Maid* is short here for "maiden," and *Master Maid* is a Norwegian way of saying "Supergirl."

Aaron Shepard

Once there was a lad named Leif. Now, Leif was a likeable fellow, and handsome to boot. But he never wanted to listen to anyone, and he always had to do things his own way.

One day he said, "Father, I'm going out into the world, where I can do things just as I like."

"My son," said his father, "your stubbornness is bound to land you in trouble. But at least take this piece of advice: Whatever you do, don't go to work for the troll."

So where do you think Leif went? Right to the house of the troll!

Leif knocked on the door, and the troll himself answered it. He was huge, and a good deal uglier than anyone you'd care to meet.

"Pardon me, sir," said Leif. "I'm looking for work."

"Are you, now?" said the troll, feeling the boy's arm. "I could use a fellow like you."

The troll led him into the stable and said, "I'm taking my goats to pasture. Since it's your first day, I won't ask much of you. Just shovel out all this dung."

"Well, that's kind of you, sir," said Leif. "You're surely easy to please!"

"But just remember one thing," said the troll. "Don't go looking through the rooms of the house, or you won't live to tell about it."

When the troll had gone, Leif said to himself, "Not look through the house? Why, that's just what I want to do!"

So Leif went through all the rooms till he came to the kitchen. And there stirring a big iron pot was the loveliest maiden he had ever seen.

"Good lord!" cried the girl. "What are you doing here?"

"I've just got a job with the troll," said Leif.

"Then heaven help you to get out of it!" said the girl. "Weren't you warned about working here?"

"I was," said Leif, "but I'm glad I came anyway, else I never would have met you!"

Well, the girl liked *that* answer, so they sat down to chat. They talked and talked and talked some more, and before the day was done, he held her hand in his.

Then the girl asked, "What did the troll tell you to do today?"

"Something easy," said Leif. "I've only to clean out the stable."

"Easy to say!" said the girl. "But if you use the pitchfork the ordinary way, ten forkfuls will fly in for every one you throw out! Now, here's what you must do. Turn the pitchfork around and shovel with the handle. Then the dung will fly out by itself."

Leif went out to the stable and took up the pitchfork. But he said to himself, "That can't be true, what she told me," and he shoveled the ordinary way. Within moments he was up to his neck in dung.

"I guess her way wouldn't hurt to try," he said. So he turned the pitchfork around and shoveled with the handle. In no time at all the dung was all out, and the stable looked as if he had scrubbed it.

As Leif started back to the house, the troll came up with the goats.

"Is the stable clean?" asked the troll.

"Tight and tidy!" said Leif, and he showed it to him.

"You never figured this out for yourself!" the troll said. "Have you been talking to my Master Maid?"

"Master Maid?" said Leif. "Now, what sort of thing might that be, sir?"

"You'll find out soon enough," said the troll.

The next morning the troll was again to go off with his goats. He told Leif, "Today I'll give you another easy job. Just go up the hill to the pasture and fetch my stallion."

"Thank you, sir," said Leif. "That won't be any trouble."

"But mind you stay out of the rooms of the house," said the troll, "or I'll make an end of you."

When the troll had gone off, Leif went right to the kitchen and sat down again with the girl whom the troll had called Master Maid.

"Didn't the troll threaten you against coming here?" she asked.

"He did," said Leif, "but he'll have to do worse to keep me away from you!"

So they talked and talked and talked some more, and before the day was done, he had his arm around her.

Then Master Maid asked, "What work did the troll give you today?"

"Nothing hard," said Leif. "I just have to fetch his stallion from the hillside."

"Yes, but how will you manage?" asked Master Maid. "It will charge at you, shooting flame from its mouth and nostrils! But here's how to do it. Take that bridle hanging by the door and hold it before you as you get near. Then the stallion will be tame as a pussycat."

So Leif threw the bridle over his shoulder and went up the hill to the pasture. But he said to himself, "That horse looks gentle enough," and he started right over to it. As soon as the stallion saw him, it charged at him, shooting flame just as Master Maid had said.

Barely in time, Leif got the bridle off his shoulder and held it before him. The stallion stopped, as tame as you please, and Leif bridled it and rode it back to the stable.

On his way out, he met the troll coming home with the goats.

"Did you bring home the stallion?" asked the troll.

"Safe and sound!" said Leif, and he showed him.

"You never figured this out for yourself!" the troll said. "Have you been talking to my Master Maid?"

"Master Maid?" said Leif. "Didn't you mention that yesterday? I'd certainly like to know what it is!"

"All in good time," said the troll.

The next morning, before the troll left with the goats, he said, "I want you to go to the mountain today and collect my tunnel tax from the fairies."

"All right, sir," said Leif. "I'm sure I can figure it out."

"But just keep out of the rooms of the house," said the troll, "or you won't make it through another day."

As soon as the troll had left, off went Leif to the kitchen and once more sat down with Master Maid.

"Aren't you the least bit afraid of the troll?" she asked.

"I am," said Leif, "but not near as much as I'm in love with you!"

So they talked and talked and talked some more, and before the day was done, she gave him a nice big kiss.

Then Master Maid asked, "What are you to do for the troll today?"

"Something simple," said Leif. "I'm to go to the mountain and collect the tunnel tax from the fairies."

"Simple if you know how!" said Master Maid. "You're lucky I'm here to tell you! Take that club that's leaning against the wall and strike it against the mountain. The rock will open up, and a fairy will ask you how much you want. Be sure to say, 'Just as much as I can carry.'"

So Leif took the club to the mountain and struck it against the side. The rock split wide open, and out came one of the fairies. Through the crack Leif could see piles and piles of silver, gold, and gems.

"I've come for the troll's tunnel tax," said Leif.

"How much do you want?" asked the fairy.

Now, Leif figured it wouldn't hurt to ask for extra and then keep some for himself. So he said, "As much as you can give me."

As soon as he said it, silver, gold, and gems came streaming out of the mountain and piled up around him. In a few moments he was nearly buried, but the treasure kept coming.

"I've changed my mind!" Leif shouted. "Just as much as I can carry!"

The pile of treasure flew back into the mountain, and the fairy handed him a sack.

As Leif arrived back, he met the troll. "Did you collect my tax?" the troll asked.

"Done and delivered!" said Leif. He opened the sack, and silver, gold, and gems overflowed onto the ground.

"You never figured this out for yourself!" the troll said. "You've been talking with my Master Maid!"

"Master Maid?" said Leif. "This is the third time you've spoken of it, sir. I wish I could see it for myself!"

"It won't be long now," said the troll.

The next morning the troll brought Leif to Master Maid. "Cut him up and throw him in the stew," he told her. "And wake me when he's done." Then he lay down on a bench and started snoring.

"Quick!" whispered Master Maid. "We must flee while we can!"

She picked up a wooden fork, a lump of salt, and a flask of water. Then she pushed Leif out the door and over to the stable. They saddled two mares and rode away at full gallop.

After awhile Leif looked behind them and saw the troll, riding like a whirlwind on his fire-breathing stallion. "We're done for!" he cried.

But Master Maid threw the wooden fork over her shoulder and shouted,

> *"Fork of wood, bless my soul.*
> *Turn to trees and stop the troll."*

The fork changed to a thick forest that blocked the troll's way.

"I know how to deal with this," said the troll, and he called out,

> *"Forest Chewer, curse her soul.*
> *Chew the forest, help the troll."*

The Forest Chewer appeared out of nowhere and devoured the trees, making a path for the troll's horse.

Leif looked back and again saw the troll. "We're lost!" he cried. But Master Maid tossed the lump of salt behind her.

"Lump of salt, bless my soul.
Grow to mountain, stop the troll."

The salt turned to a craggy mountain, and the troll again had to stop. "I know how to handle this too!" he said.

"Mountain Cruncher, curse her soul.
Crunch the mountain, help the troll."

The Mountain Cruncher appeared and bored a tunnel, straight through the mountain.

Meanwhile Leif and Master Maid came to a sea, where they found a sailboat tied up. They left the horses, boarded the boat, and sailed for the far shore.

They were halfway across when the troll rode up to the water. "I can take care of this as well!" he said.

"Water Sucker, curse her soul.
Suck the water, help the troll."

The Water Sucker appeared and started drinking up the sea. Soon the boat was scraping bottom.

"It's the end of us!" cried Leif. But Master Maid took out her flask.

"Drop of water, bless my soul.
Fill the sea and stop the troll."

She poured a single drop overboard, and the drop of water filled the sea.

"Drink it up! Drink it up!" raged the troll. But not another drop could the Water Sucker drink, and Leif and Master Maid landed safe on the other shore.

It wasn't long then till Leif had Master Maid home, and not long again till they had a wedding. But when the minister asked Master Maid if she'd love, honor, and obey, Leif told him, "Never mind that! It's best if *I* obey *her.*"

And he did—which is why they lived happily ever after.